SHIT LONDON

Dedicated to Gordon – he would have loved the anarchic sense of humour.

Published in the United Kingdom in 2011 by
Portico Books
10 Southcombe Street
London
W14 0RA

An imprint of Anova Books Company Ltd

All photographs printed with permission. None of the photography in this book has been altered, or Photoshopped, in any way.

ISBN 978-190755-43-4-6

A CIP catalogue record for this book is available from the British Library.

10 9 8 7 6 5 4 3

Printed and bound by 1010 Printing International Ltd, China

This book can be ordered direct from the publisher at www.anovabooks.com

For more *Shit London* stuff why not head over to www.shitlondon.co.uk, or be part of the group on Facebook. Go on, you know you want to.

SHIT LONDON

SNAPSHOTS OF A CITY ON THE EDGE

PATRICK DALTON

PORTICO

When a man is tired of London, he is tired of life.

Samuel Johnson (dead)

INTRODUCTION

London. Capital of culture, fashion, finance and thinking. A city where the ancient meets the modern and the chic, let's be honest, meets the shit. Despite the government's best efforts to smarten up England's scruffy old-man of a city before the 2012 Olympics, local boroughs of immeasurable crumminess still stand defiant in the path of progress. Hidden behind the architectural delights and the history exists a world that proves London will always be a world-class city of bad taste, worse spellings and general rubbishness. But as a city, London isn't shit, it just has shitness *in* it ... and in that shitness it excels.

Everyday, Londoners are surrounded by pure acts of comedy (some intentional, some not) but through the sheer weight of visual stimuli presented to them they are unable to register any of it. Instead, it remains the flotsam and jetsam of city life, the overlooked minutiae, the ill conceived, the charmingly inept and the basest of base. And it comes in many disguises too. From random acts of sign vandalism to the dirty joke fingered on the back of a van, or just plain awful shop names, it's all there – modern folk art of the most transient kind.

But aside from being funny, these photographs also capture a city in flux – and a world that is rapidly vanishing. The increasing homogenisation of the high street is slowly turning our urban spaces into identikit joy voids.

Above all, what the *Shit London* philosophy hopefully demonstrates is that beneath the smooth veneer of our digital age there is still a human heart beating, and the bygone age of independent shops and community that people wistfully refer to might not have disappeared just yet. It still exists everywhere if you choose to notice it.

Unconsciously, a few years ago, I began taking random photos of the city after getting my first digital camera. Whenever I saw something that caught my eye I would snap it, and being somewhat of a hoarder, I soon amassed quite a collection of hilarious/disturbing photos. That's when the idea of *Shit London* hit me.

I now actively seek photos of a strange nature, crossing the city in search of oddities, curiosities and weirdness ... an urban safari, if you will. Through these expeditions I have got to see the city in a completely new light – how it links up above ground without the help of the Tube. It's been like learning 'the Knowledge', except instead of becoming educated with a helpful, mental map of London's road network, I'm stuck with a useless A–Z of crappy fried-chicken shops, vandalised street signs and the best places to see knob graffiti.

So, now that you've bought the book, if you see a strange figure walking the city streets clutching a camera, his head jerking from the gutter to strange shop signs, camera flashing, then that could be me ... but please, do not stop and say hello. This is London after all, I'll probably think you're trying to mug me.

Patrick Dalton, London, April 2011

Railway sidings, Wimbledon

Just careless, Hackney

Winkfield Road, Haringey

Bike crime scene

Northwold Road, Stoke Newington

Street sofa

No lion, no witch, just wardrobe

Outside a Primary School, Bethnal Green

Pigeons rebrand noodle restaurant, Elephant and Castle

Adapted poster, Finsbury Park Station

Nursery School mural, Mare Street, Hackney

Papal warning,
Kensington High Street

Dalston Market

Well Street, Hackney

Gun Street, Poplar

Safer than knife crime, Camden

Dog poo vigilante action, Camden

He's back, and apparently a Tory, Wimbledon Village

Blood-splattered poster, Wimbledon

Eerily prophetic campaign poster, Shoreditch

Failed sign, Shepherds Bush Green

Tarmac sick note, Leytonstone

Pigeonless wings, Charing Cross

Contradictory door

London Road, Morden

Enticing offer, Kentish Town

'Polite' notice #1
Tooting Broadway market

Tour des Londres, Wardour Street, Soho

Bullet-holed bus, Route 29

Insecure van, Leyton

Wandsworth Bridge Road

Simba, Great Portland Street

Dickheads, Highbury and Islington Tube station

Hoo Ha!, Wood Green

Geese graffiti, Clapham Common

Insensitive advertising,
Edgware Road

Vague optimism, Leather Lane, Holborn

Sunday morning debris,
Hungerford Bridge

'Polite' notice #2, Tooting

Albion Road, Stoke Newington

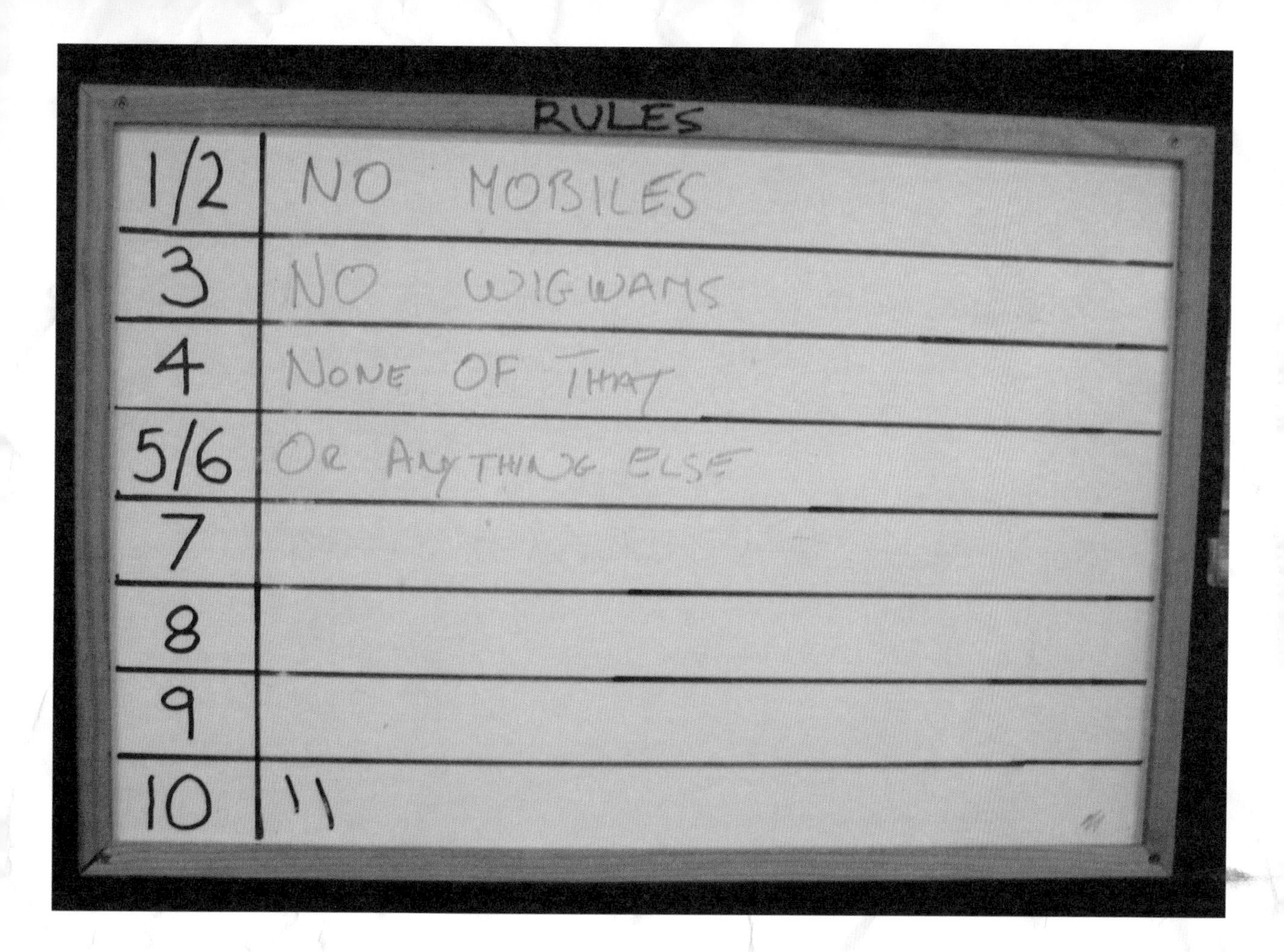

South Bank book market

Mare Street, Hackney

Spatial awareness

High Road, Leyton

Sydenham Road, Sydenham

- lickin' bad, Elephant and Castle

Cruel high-visibility vests, Charing Cross

*Lock, Stock...*inspired sentiment, Wimbledon Chase

Entire borough shanked, Hackney

Inaccurate sign-writing – triple threat

Bethnal Green Station

SPECIAL EDITION

LONDON BLAMED FOR JACKSON DEATH

London Evening Standard

TOMORROW'S NEWS TODAY

Victoria Station

Fan tribute, Finsbury Park

Tooting Bec Station

Portal to the afterlife, Mile End

York Way, Islington

Efes café, Alaska Street

Hornsey Road, Islington

Blenheim Crescent, Notting Hill

Recruitment poster, Hackney Wick

Sunday sickness, Hackney

Graffitied campaign poster, Whitechapel

Welcome to Dream Land, Wentworth Street

Oxymorons, Hackney

Knob graffiti, Highbury and Islington Tube Station

Seven Sisters Road, Manor House

Dalston Lane, Hackney

Crouch End

Morden Road, Wimbledon

Loitering's OK, but no hanging out, Peter Street, Soho

Headless man, night bus, N77

Drive fail, Crystal Palace

Hair product penis,
Stoke Newington

Play nice, Islington

Cliff Road, Camden

Vegetable-gun-waterfall mural, Putney

Carden, City Road

Time Out panics newsagent, Fulham

Pub toilet, Borough

Nice mural, badly placed, Chelsea and Westminster Hospital car park

Eeyore, Hammersmith

Carnival rubbish island, Notting Hill

Heygate Estate, Elephant and Castle

Waxing man, Regent Street

Dolphin football, Mare Street

Neal Street, Covent Garden

Fish 'n' Chip shop, Waterloo

Vintage clothes shop, Whitechapel

Knob heart, Brick Lane

Police notice, Villers Street

EVERY TUESDAY
ROBOT
FIREMAN'S
FIRST TEST
South London
PRESS
Your local Newspaper

Bankside

Karmic threat

Clearly ignored sign,
South Kensington

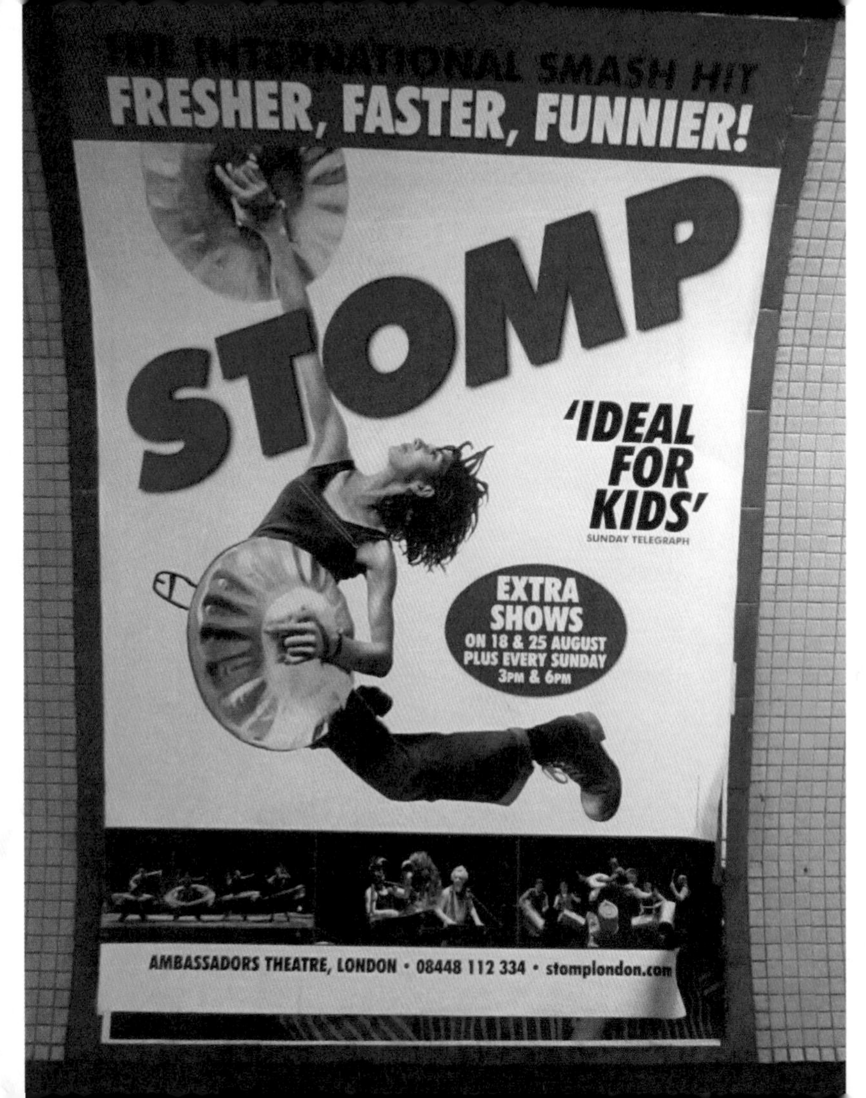

Stomp cock,
Highbury and Islington

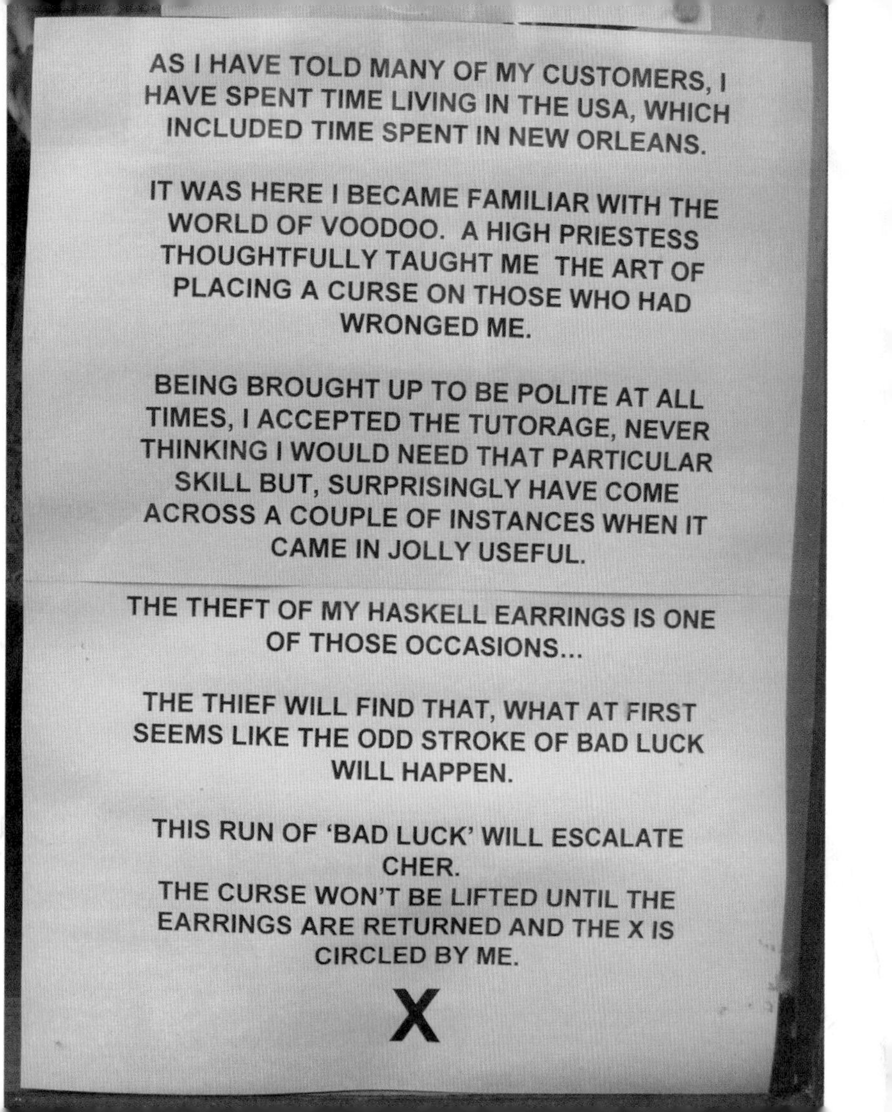

AS I HAVE TOLD MANY OF MY CUSTOMERS, I HAVE SPENT TIME LIVING IN THE USA, WHICH INCLUDED TIME SPENT IN NEW ORLEANS.

IT WAS HERE I BECAME FAMILIAR WITH THE WORLD OF VOODOO. A HIGH PRIESTESS THOUGHTFULLY TAUGHT ME THE ART OF PLACING A CURSE ON THOSE WHO HAD WRONGED ME.

BEING BROUGHT UP TO BE POLITE AT ALL TIMES, I ACCEPTED THE TUTORAGE, NEVER THINKING I WOULD NEED THAT PARTICULAR SKILL BUT, SURPRISINGLY HAVE COME ACROSS A COUPLE OF INSTANCES WHEN IT CAME IN JOLLY USEFUL.

THE THEFT OF MY HASKELL EARRINGS IS ONE OF THOSE OCCASIONS...

THE THIEF WILL FIND THAT, WHAT AT FIRST SEEMS LIKE THE ODD STROKE OF BAD LUCK WILL HAPPEN.

THIS RUN OF 'BAD LUCK' WILL ESCALATE CHER.
THE CURSE WON'T BE LIFTED UNTIL THE EARRINGS ARE RETURNED AND THE X IS CIRCLED BY ME.

X

Shoplifter curse,
Wimbledon Village

Sports shop window display,
Walworth Road

Pat Butcher's wardrobe, Wentworth Street

Pelican crossing,
Clerkenwell Road

Amorous Graffiti, Hackney

Cruel graffiti, Kensal Rise

Walkers Court, Soho

The circle of life, Camden Stable Market

Backstage toilet, Brick Lane

DISCOUNT THEARTER
TICKETS
'THIS BLOCKBUSTER MUSICAL
IS FABULOUSLY ENTERTAINING
WICKED
APOLLO VICTORIA THEATRE
Calendar
Girls
by
Tim Firth
NOËL COWARD THEATRE
SMOKE SHOP
THE TAPPIT HEN
WINE HOUSE
DAVENPORTS
MAGIC
SHOP & STUDIO
Ask Cora
WHAT'S INSTORE
WEIDER HEALTH
& FITNESS

ACKNOWLEDGEMENTS

In no particular order I'd like to thank ...

Sam Twiddy, Tina Smith, Fred Marcucci, Ben Coupland, Mat McNerney, Tom 'Pizzaboy' Blanks, Kerry Flynn, Emily Hope, Jack McGinity, Tiph Shipman, David Braithwaite, Simon Chamberlain, Tom and Peter Warwick, Dan Alexander, Christian Aeschliman, Joe Gardiner, all my brilliant friends and family (you know who you are), CA Halpin and The Outside World Gallery, Canon Cameras, all the incredibly witty members of the *Shit London* Facebook group who keep it great, The Captain, Malcolm Croft at Portico for getting it so completely, Denny, Nora, Mum and Dad for everything and, finally, for anyone who ever hung around waiting for me whilst I took a photograph of something ridiculous. I'm sorry.

CONTRIBUTING PHOTOGRAPHERS

Zoe Anspach, Alva Bernadine, This Country, Chrissie Dalziel, Gary Dempsey, Ollie Downward, Paddy Duncan, Britt Foe Cormack, Emma Gilchrist, Elliot Goldner, CA Halpin, Siobhan Hennessey, Paul Howard,Tamsin Hull, Deb Israel, Richard Jones, Ben Kelly, Araminta Knox, Ed Lomas, Arkem Mark, Andrew McEwan, Luca Pedrazzi, Nick Pope, David Rostron, Mel Saunders, Stu Sibley,Tom Sweet, Brennan Till, Ben Topiman, Phillip Warburton.